The battle in England!

The quarrel in Byzantium!

My second scar from Jorvik!

The accident at the summer party!

For Björn Desmond Manning with our love

What a Viking! *was made on loaction in Sweden and England in 1999.*
Thanks to: Lars Holmblad at the National History Museum, Stockholm; Kristina Granström;
Mart and Bosse; Olav Trätelja; Odin, Thor, Frey and Freya; Sigtuna Museum; Birka;
Jorvick Museum – and the island of Lindisfarne.

Consultant: Lars Homblad, the National History Museum, Stockholm

This edition published in 2000 by
Franklin Watts, 96 Leonard Street
London EC2A 4XD

Franklin Watts Australia
14 Mars Road, Lane Cove
NSW 2006

ISBN 0 7496 3972 5

First published in Sweden by Raben and Sjögren Bokförlag
under the title *Vilken viking!*

Text and artwork © Mick Manning and Brita Granström 2000
A CIP catalogue record for this book is available from the British Library

Printed in Denmark

WHAT A VIKING!

MICK MANNING & BRITA GRANSTRÖM

W

FRANKLIN WATTS

LONDON • SYDNEY

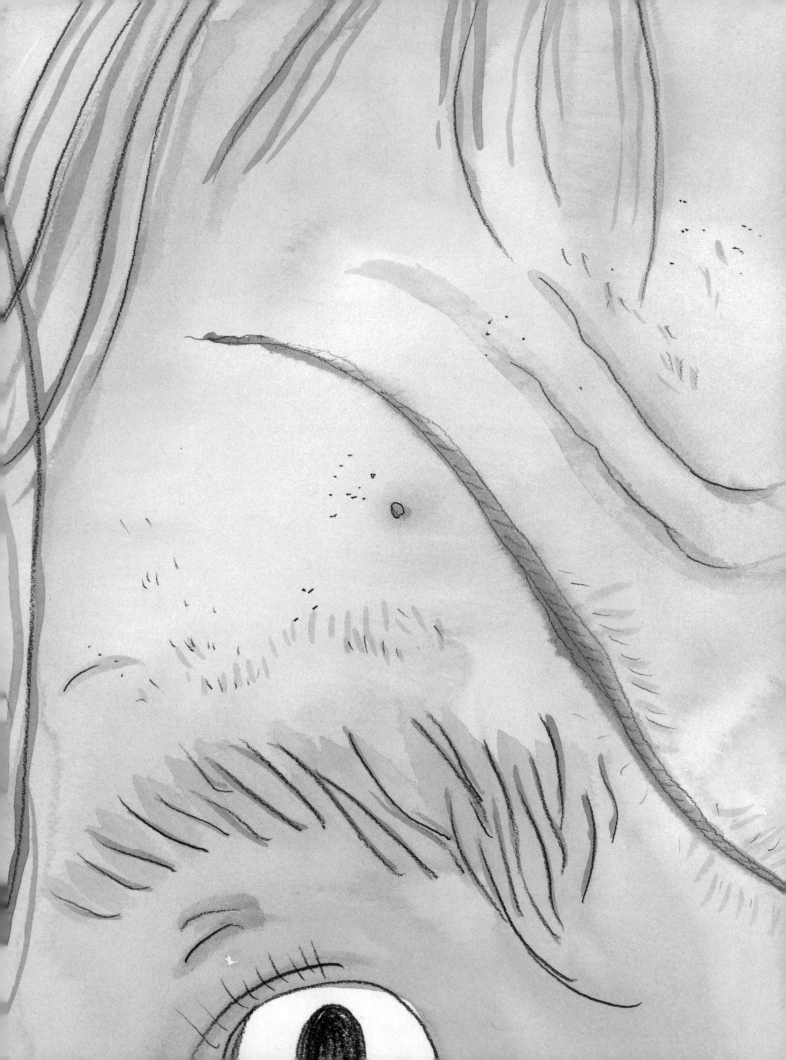

Look! What do you see?
Rivers winding through valleys?
Caves where dragons live?
Or a treasure map perhaps?
These are my scars . . .
my life story!

Here I am chop-chopping wood on a peaceful sunny day. But long ago I was a different sort of chopper …

I was a Viking!

Vikings came from Sweden, Norway and Denmark. They raided, explored and settled in many other countries.

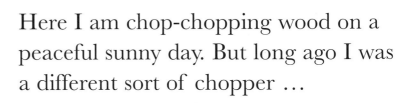

The English thought Vikings were very clean – they had a bath every Saturday _and_ combed their hair!

Grill iron

This clever shape cooks food evenly – just like the ring on an electric stove.

A Viking baby's drinking cup made of wood

I grew up in Birka – that was the busiest town in Sweden in those days. But, by the age of thirteen, I was bored!

I was fed up with being called "little Björn", fed up with unloading barrels of herring for my uncle and fed up living at home with my bossy sister.

← Viking keys hung from belts and chains.

Sails were made with the oily, waterproof wool of Viking sheep.

Viking ships had oars for rowing into harbour or in case the wind dropped.

One morning I saw a wonderful sight …
Gliding into harbour like a golden eagle among the seagulls was a dragon-headed, red-and-white-sailed sea serpent! How could a ship look so beautiful? That very day I told my uncle where to stuff his herrings, kissed my mum goodbye and joined the crew – just like that!

Vikings had different sorts of boats - cargo boats, rowing boats and warships.

We sailed over the horizon and far away …
I grew taller, stronger and uglier every year!
I wasn't little Björn any longer! I loved to smell
the sea and feel the wind on my hairy, young face.
I had shipmates from Sweden, Denmark and Norway
and, for a while, raiding adventures became a way of
life for us.

Vikings kept their things in the chests they sat on or under the deck.

A Viking tool chest

At sea Vikings ate dried fish, meat, fruit, oats and hard bread.

I helped burn down a few churches – and I nicked my share of silver too! Like many other Vikings I didn't know any better in those days. We had a whole team of Gods to help us: Odin, the one eyed Wizard; Thor who killed giants with a magic hammer; Frey and Freya who made both our crops and babies grow! Tyr the God of war and the Valkyrie maidens who carried Viking heroes to Valhalla … Oh, and let's not forget Loki – he was always up to no good.

Vikings chopped up their treasure so they could share it out.

Hacksilver

Vikings wore symbols of their favourite gods. Some wore christian crosses too — the more gods the better that's how they saw it!

viking cross

Odins spear

Two Thor's hammers

cross from England found in Sweden

Frey's steel

Hacksilver was often made into new jewellery, like this snake ...

A comb from Byzantium

A bronze flask brought home to Sweden

We didn't always stay with the same boat. One year I joined a boat sailing East. We sailed across monster-infested seas and rowed down winding rivers until we reached a far away land called Byzantium. What sweet memories that word brings back! I got into some adventures there, in fact it was where I got my first scar …

Arab coins were often taken home and used as jewellery.

After a year or two living in Byzantium, I sailed West to Dublin. What a town! Shiploads of silk and gold. Markets full of leatherworkers, shoemakers, combmakers, jewellers – and slavetraders …

I got a proper job in Dublin – as a bodyguard for the Earl of Orkney's kids, Tovi and Toki.

You might call that babysitting – well maybe – but this babysitter carried his axe at all times!

You could buy all these things in Viking Dublin...

bone ice-skates

leather shoes

wooden toys

a ring pin for your cloak

or amber beads

A Viking toilet was a deep hole in the ground with a seat on top.

Viking poo found in Dublin

Tweezers and ear scoop found down a Viking toilet

Many Vikings had tummy bugs because their toilets leaked into their drinking water!

And I soon had to use it! I'd only left the kids for a minute – even Vikings have to use the toilet! When I got back a slavetrader had grabbed them. He was a big bully dressed in sealskin and he claimed I either had to pay him or fight to get the kids back … So, guess what I did? "Fish breath" was more used to whipping slaves than fighting, he didn't last long. I got a scar for my trouble and my reputation as the best bodyguard money could buy! Oh yes, and I set all his slaves free as well …

Viking duels were fought on a cloak. If you stepped off or lost the fight, the winner got all your property!

The stars at night and this sun compass found in Greenland helped the Vikings discover America a thousand years ago.

This viking pin was found in America.

One spring a crowd of us set sail for new adventures. Some ships sailed North to Scotland and Iceland – and who knows where else! Others sailed home to Scandinavia …

Me? I sailed to join Olaf's army – we were going to conquer England!

A few weeks later I had survived a battle!
Hundreds of people fighting and shouting and chopping
at each other. We won, but my head got split wide open
by a sword cut. That's how I got my third scar.

A Viking's favourite weapons...

spear

battle axe

skulls found in
England show how
Vikings died in
battle...

sword

arrow

Smiths made tools and weapons – and some made jewellery. If a smith burned his hand, he plunged it into a bucket of pee – it was a sort of antiseptic!

Jorvik was the centre of Viking England. Lots of merchants and artists lived there – and robbers too, so it was there that I hired out my services as a bodyguard again.

One night I was guarding a money lender when we got ambushed by two "cut throats". In a couple of blows I knocked one of them out! But the second bandit was quick as a snake. First he slashed my face, then he stabbed my arm! My blood flowed like water from a leaky barrel! Luckily he slipped in the muddy street and we made our escape in the moonlight …

A few years later I met Thora. She was the village stone lifting champion – and when she started sending me love letters carved in runes I knew I'd met my match! We soon settled down together and like lots of other Vikings I became a farmer.

← The runes on this bone say "Kiss me"!

Vikings didn't use forks – just their own knife and sometimes a wooden spoon.

Vikings were good farmers and they loved feasts!

All Vikings like parties, and that's where I got my sixth scar – at a midsummer festival.

There was wrestling, axe throwing, stone lifting, games for the kids … But even Vikings can have accidents and, during the archery contest, someone missed the target and I got the silly donkey's arrow stuck in my hairy backside!

Vikings loved summer sports. In the winter they played board games and told stories about their gods and heroes.

←This chess piece was found on a Scottish island.

So, now you've heard my story, take another look at
my scars – what do you see? Rivers winding through
valleys? Caves where dragons live?
Or a treasure map perhaps …

Dogs, cats, hawks and ferrets were common
viking pets – they were useful for hunting too!

Helpful words

Art — Vikings were great artists carving stone and wood and making jewellery, shoes, clothing and everyday objects like combs in their own "Viking style".

Byzantium — a huge empire in the Middle East. Its capital was Constantinople (now Istanbul). Some Vikings worked there guarding the Emperor.

Combs — were important not just to look tidy but to get rid of lice and nits, common pests in hair and beards!

Cut throat — a name for a robber.

Dublin — Viking-age market town, now the capital of the Republic of Ireland. A Viking longship found at Roskilde in Denmark was originally built in Dublin!

Earscoop — Vikings cleaned their ears and kept the wax to use as a moisturiser for chapped hands in the winter!

Frej and Freja — Viking Gods that made the seasons come and go. They also made all living things grow.

Jorvik — The most important town in Viking-age England – now it's called York.

Language — Most Scandinavian words, about half of all English words and many French ones are Viking.

Money lender — a person who lends people money which they pay back to him later including some extra money called interest.

Odin — The most powerful Viking God who swapped an eye for magic powers. His ravens, Hugin and Munin, told him all that went on in the world – past, present and future.

Place name endings — like thwaite (clearing), holm (islet or mound), sta (place), thorpe (farm) and by (village) are signs Vikings once lived there.

Runes — Viking letters that could be easily carved on wood, stone or bone.

Saxons — the people living in England at that time.

Slaves — were people sold by force to be the property of some-one else. No one wanted to be made a slave – the Viking name Karl actually means "free man".

Thor — was the Viking's favourite God (they called him Tor). He rode in a chariot pulled by goats – making thunder and lightning.

Tummy bugs — come from drinking dirty water. Vikings might have had a bath every week – but like everyone else then they had bugs living in their tummy and nits in their hair.

Valhalla — was Odin's feasting hall. Half the Vikings that died in battle went there – the others went to Frey and Freya's place.

Vikings — the Viking-age started in the 8th Century and the word "Viking" began as the word for sea raiders but soon became a name for all the people who came from Sweden, Denmark and Norway at that time. Vikings later settled in other countries, including Scotland, Ireland, England, Iceland, Greenland, France, Russia and even America for a short time.

Slipped in some cow muck!

Bitten by a ferret!